Not Safe

Not Safe

Danuta Reah

CRIME EXPRESS

Not Safe
by Danuta Reah

Published in 2011 by Crime Express
Crime Express is an imprint of
Five Leaves Publications,
PO Box 8786, Nottingham NG1 9AW
www.fiveleaves.co.uk

ISBN: 978 1 907869 09 9

© Danuta Reah, 2011

Crime Express 11

Five Leaves acknowledges financial support
from Arts Council England

Five Leaves is represented by Turnaround
and distributed by Central Books.

Cover design: Gavin Morris

Typeset and design;
Four Sheets Design and Print

Printed by Imprint Digital in Great Britain

The night was cold. The temperature had been dropping all day and now a sleety rain was falling, making the paving stones gleam in the lamp light. Amir's bag cut into his shoulder, reminding him of the days when he was plumper, when Nargus used to laugh and tell him he would grow fat and she wouldn't love him any more.

"I'll be fat, but I'll be rich," he'd told her. "You'll still love me." She'd punched his shoulder in mock outrage. He wondered where she was and what had happened to her, then pushed the thought away. *Not here. Not now.*

He hitched the bag higher. He needed it, heavy though it was. It contained all his possessions: a change of clothes, a sleeping bag, a wind-up torch, his books and his Q'ran, some tea bags and some biscuits.

He sighed and let the bag slide to the ground, straightening up and stretching to ease his spine. The dual carriageway behind him was still busy with the roar of traffic and the rattle of heavy lorries racing past. In front of him, the steep hill vanished into the shadow of a railway viaduct. The street, lined with industrial sheds and old brick warehouses, was empty.

He'd already been walking for 20 minutes and he had at least another 20 minutes' fast walking ahead of him before he reached the old church where the night shelter was based. The hill looked formidable and his energy was fading. He could walk back into the city, try and find a place to sleep – the bus station, a shop doorway – but places like that weren't safe. Late at night, the streets were the home of drunks, drug users and the police.

He really didn't want to run into the police.

He switched on his phone, using up valuable charge, in case there was a message from Tehreem. Tehreem had a room and sometimes, against the rules of the National Asylum Seekers Support, let Amir spread his sleeping bag on the floor, but he hadn't called.

Amir could feel the cold creeping through his layers of clothing. He summoned his resources and picked the bag up again. It was the shelter or the streets, and the streets weren't an option.

He pushed himself into movement, and encouraged his weary legs with promises: *nearly there, nearly there.*

The sound of footsteps broke his concentration. Years of street living made him move quickly. He shoved his phone into his inside pocket, checking automatically for the plastic edge of his identity card. The phone was his lifeline and the card gave him what few rights remained to him. He backed against the wall and waited.

The footsteps approached rapidly, and as the person behind him drew closer, there was enough light from the moon for Amir to see her face.

It was a young woman. He didn't remember seeing her before. There was no danger of a mugging here. Her footsteps slowed as she walked towards him. He realised that she knew who he was and had been following him. He waited.

"Hello. I see you at the place, the... Nadifa." She meant Nadifa's House, a small support centre that gave what help it could to destitute asylum seekers like Amir. Amir worked there as a volunteer.

"Are you... a place. I need a place. To sleep." Her English was heavily accented, and she was struggling to find the words. "Could I... come with you? Or stay with you? If... On the street, I meant."

Amir hesitated. He didn't want to be responsible for her. In this kind of life, it was hard enough to take care of yourself. There was very little left for anyone else. He shook his head slowly, about to say no, but something stopped the word from coming. She was very young, still in her teens.

Her face was pinched with the cold. She was wearing jeans and a jacket, far too thin for the winter night. The beads in her hair clacked together as she pushed it back from her face, and he saw traces of bruising high on her cheek.

"I can... If you let me stay with you, you can..." She struggled to find the words. "...fuck," she said. "You can... with me."

Amir wondered what had happened to her since she had arrived in this country to bring her to this. The weight of responsibility settled round his shoulders. When he spoke to her, he switched to Arabic and kept his words formal to remove any possibility of misunderstanding. "No. Please. My sister, there is no need." He was puzzled. Nadifa's House had limited resources, but they wouldn't leave a young and vulnerable girl like this on the streets. "Why didn't you ask at Nadifa's House?"

She looked away, and didn't answer. He tried

again. "You must go back to them. Tomorrow. They can help you."

She nodded, still not meeting his gaze. He wasn't sure if she would listen to him, and for now, she was his responsibility.

She was too young to be out on her own. The shelter he was heading for didn't offer any accommodation for women, but there might be something they could do. If not, maybe he should stay with her on the street. He didn't want to do that. The cold was eating into his bones, and the thought of warmth was irresistible. "I know a place. They might help you."

She chewed her lip, looking round the dark road. "Where?"

"Not far."

Her eyes went past him, to the hill behind them. "Not the street?"

"Not the street. Come on. We should go. It's too cold to stay here." He began moving, and after a moment, she followed him. He looked at the girl trudging up the hill beside him, trying to plan ahead. There was every chance she would be turned away, then... what was he going to do?

It all depended who was on duty. If it was his friend Andre Mutombo ... Mutombo knew what it was to have no home. He was a refugee from the Democratic Republic of Congo. Unlike Amir, his claim for refugee status had been accepted and for the time being, he was allowed to stay, along with his two small boys. Amir had met him at Nadifa's House where they both did voluntary work. The two men were good friends. Amir switched on his phone, trying to work out how much credit he had left, and keyed in Andre's number.

As if in response, a phone rang. The girl jumped and took it out of her pocket. She checked the screen and switched it off, shaking her head and looking around nervously.

Andre wasn't answering. There was no point in leaving a message. Amir would find out if he was on duty soon enough.

The girl wrapped her arms round herself, and the small bag she was carrying slipped out of her hands. He picked it up and gave it back to her, realising that her fingers must be numb with cold. He hesitated – it was everyone for himself in this life – then pulled off his jacket and wrapped it round her shoulders. "Come on."

The girl's steps became slower and more reluctant as he led the way. Amir tried to conceal his impatience. She was cold and she was probably ill. She seemed frightened as well.

They were walking through residential streets now, rows of red brick terraces in the intermittent street light. The pavement was uneven, the flagstones gleaming as a thin rain began to fall. A dog barked somewhere close by, and the girl shrank against him.

Their slow pace meant it was almost half an hour before they reached the shelter. It stood at the top of a steep, narrow street. The girl's grip on his arm dragged as she moved, step by reluctant step.

The shelter was half way up the hill, barely visible behind a wall, the gate opening onto a small yard. The sign outside said, "St Barnabas Church Hall," with a faded list of opening times below. He was aware of her footsteps slowing even more. "Is this…?" Her voice was a whisper.

It was just gone 11. As Amir watched, a light came on and the doors opened. Like magic, people emerged from the shadows round about, from where they had been waiting in the cold. He squinted, trying to focus, and thought he saw a tall, broad silhouette move across the window. Andre Mutombo. Relief flooded through him. He could hand the girl over and rest. "Come on."

Before he could react, she turned on her heel and fled back down the road into the shadows, vanishing with his coat into the night.

"Hey!" He moved to follow her, then realised the weight of the bag would make it impossible for him to catch her up. He dithered, moved the way she'd gone, then stopped, muttering a curse under his breath. The lure of shelter was irresistible. She'd be OK, she'd got his coat. She wouldn't freeze. He might. There was nothing else he could do.

Now he was here, he allowed himself to feel the cold, and to acknowledge he was hungry. He had food in his bag.

Unlike the girl.

He was frozen, but he had warmth and shelter waiting for him.

Unlike the girl.

The shelter didn't offer much. He would have to unroll his sleeping bag onto the floor. He'd be out on the street in the cold again at eight the next morning with the long walk back into the city in front of him and another day ahead, but he could sleep safely.

Unlike the girl.

He crossed the road to the entrance and rang the bell. Andre's bulk filled the small window, and the door opened. "Amir!" Andre gestured him in with a companionable arm. "The kettle's on. I've got the chess board set out if you…"

Amir shook his head. "I can't stay. I have to do something. Can I leave this?" He indicated the bag. "And come back later…?"

"How much later? Radcliffe's in charge tonight. He might not let you in." Radcliffe was the minister of St Barnabas Church. "Are you in trouble?"

"It isn't me. There's a girl I'm worried about. I met her on my way here. She doesn't have anywhere to go. Is there somewhere you could put her, just for tonight?"

Mutombo stood in silence, assessing the situation. The rules of the shelter were clear: no women. "How old?"

"Young. Seventeen? Maybe younger."

Mutombo had had a daughter. He never talked about what had happened to her. "There's the store room. No one goes in there at night. She'll have to be quiet. If he finds her..." If Radcliffe found her, they were all in trouble. Destitute asylum seekers were not wanted, not even in this part of the city where most of the people were first and second generation immigrants. The church needed little excuse to close the shelter down.

A car pulled up in the road, and a man got out of the passenger side. He leaned forward to speak to the driver, then reached into the back seat to collect something. "Radcliffe," Mutombo said.

Amir nodded. He moved into the shadows of the small car park as the tall shape of the minister straightened up and he headed towards the door. "Andre!" Amir heard him say, then his voice was drowned by the car engine as it pulled away. Wrapping his scarf more tightly round his neck, Amir went back the way he had come.

The wind was rising now, a thin, cutting wind that blew needles of ice into his face and cut through his clothes. No coat. He had no coat. He shouldn't have listened to the girl. He should have walked away. He should be in the shelter now drinking hot tea and playing chess with Andre and Jim Radcliffe.

His feet were hurting, and the sleet was turning into snow, the flakes whirling in the darkness, making him stumble and stagger as if he were drunk. He knew he must be cold, but he couldn't feel it any more. *Stupid, stupid.* Nargus' voice reproached him as she wrapped something round him. *Lie down, you must rest.* He was tired, so tired and the blanket was so warm...

He stumbled, and he was back on the dark street, the blank eyes of the windows watching him. He was going to kill himself like this. He should go back to the shelter.

Her face had been thin, drained of colour, but still the face of a pretty young girl, a girl who should be with her family, not offering her body to strangers on the streets of this country that had refused her sanctuary.

He didn't know where Nargus was, if she was waiting for him, if she was even alive. Maybe, somewhere in the world, she too was depending on the kindness of strangers. He couldn't abandon the girl.

He was better than this. It was all he had left. He was better than the people who refused help to a young girl in trouble, he was better than the men who used her desperation for their own ends. He had to find her.

He stood at the top of the road, his hands tucked under his arms, trying to decide what to do. She had run away. She had looked – not angry, but scared. Ever since her phone had rung... Something had frightened her. He trudged on.

He was back on the road where they had first met. Below him, the road vanished into the shadows of the railway viaduct. On the far side of the valley, streetlamps made ribbons of light. Silhouettes of trees lined the distant hill tops.

There was no sign of the girl. Sheds and warehouses loomed above him. They were solidly locked – she couldn't have got into one of them, and they had no doorways to offer even minimal shelter against the cold.

It was hopeless. She could be anywhere. He took his phone out of his pocket and switched it on. The battery still showed two bars, and he could charge it at the shelter. He hesitated again, then pressed the call button. *Dialling number ... calling ...* He was about to lift the phone to his ear when he heard the sound, faint but clear in the cold air. Somewhere close by, a phone was ringing.

***

It was after midnight. Sophie Shepherd tried to swear as she stumbled up the long hill that led away from town. Her feet kept turning in her shoes – spiky heeled sandals that had seemed so cool when she put them on. She didn't have the breath left for swearing. She'd promised she'd be back by midnight. Her dad was going to kill her.

Her face felt stiff where the tears had dried. The wind was blowing now, thin and cutting, finding its way through the fabric of her dress.

Nathan. She wanted to kill him. She wanted to be dead, lying there in the cold so that he and Becky would be sorry when they found her, when they came running after her to say they were wrong, it had all been a mistake. But it hadn't. She knew what she had seen, Nathan and that slag all over each other in the passageway outside the bar.

It was the cold that was making her eyes water and her nose run. She rubbed an angry arm across her eyes, sniffed and looked up the hill in front of her. It stretched away into the shadows of the viaduct. The road was empty. No one came this way.

She'd stormed out of the club, forgetting she didn't have any money for a taxi, forgetting how cold it was, waiting for Nathan's voice, *Hey, Sophe, come back*. He hadn't noticed. He hadn't fucking noticed her standing there, him with his hand down Becky's front and his tongue down her throat.

She needed to pee. She kept walking, trying to keep her thighs pressed together, but it was no good. She couldn't hold on till she got home. There was no one around, but she couldn't just pee here, out in the road. She walked further up the hill, the tears starting to trickle out of her eyes again, when she saw the gennel. It was invisible until you were on top of it.

She stumbled into the gap between the high buildings, pulling down her tights and knickers. She crouched down and relaxed, letting the warm liquid flow out of her, splashing up from the ground onto her shoes.

Her gaze darted nervously around as she took

stock of her surroundings. She was in a narrow alleyway, the brick walls high above her glinting where the moonlight caught them. Down here, at street level, it was pitch black. She put her hands against the rough surface of the brick to help her balance, recoiling as they pressed against something clammy and wet. *Moss*, she told himself. *Weeds growing out from the wall.* She groped in her bag for a tissue to dry herself, then froze.

In the dim shadows along the gennel, she could hear something moving.

Rats.

She stumbled to her feet, forgetting about the sticky dampness of her crotch, the tangle of clothing around her knees, her hands scraping against the rough brick of the wall. Her legs were caught and before she could stop herself, she fell, her face smacking into the ground, her bag flying out of her hand, its contents scattering.

And there was a faint light now, shining from somewhere beyond her, showing her things she didn't want to see: a shape huddled on the ground, a face, with a trickle of blood running from the corner of the mouth, blank eyes staring at her.

Then she realised there was someone else there, someone who had been crouched over the figure on the ground coming slowly to his feet. He was looking at her. He was looking right at her.

The light was extinguished, and she was alone with the thing on the ground, alone with the man in the alley, trying to get her breath, trying to scream for her dad in the darkness.

"...and then this week, Chris Moyles live from Card..."

Tina Barraclough groped for the radio switch and silenced the manic cheerfulness of the presenter. She fell out of bed, waiting for the headache to strike. No headache. She hadn't been drinking last night. She hadn't had a drink for over two months.

A two-minute blast from the shower woke her up. She told herself she didn't want a cigarette, and went through to the kitchen, towelling her hair.

Tina's flat was in one of the many new blocks that had shot up in the city centre during the boom. It was a convenient place for a young single woman to live. OK, her view was the pub across the road, but what could you do with a view apart from look at it? They had hanging baskets in summer. That was enough green for her.

She could hear the sound of impatient horns,

and the clank and clatter of the trams as they wove their way through the gathering congestion. She needed to get moving. She put a cup of last night's coffee into the microwave and started pulling on some clothes.

The microwave pinged. The coffee was bitter but it was hot. She came alert as the caffeine hit her and her hand reached automatically for the packet of cigarettes that was no longer on the shelf by the cooker.

She pushed a couple of slices of bread into the toaster, and did her hair while she was waiting, dragging a brush through the heavy mass and confining it in a clip. The image in the mirror looked businesslike but severe, so she pulled a few curls free. She pulled on a black skirt and a red jersey, and slipped her feet into the Jimmy Choos she'd bought in the sales, all red shiny leather and straps. This would be their first outing. Tart chic.

They weren't designed for patrolling the streets, but she wouldn't need to do much walking. For the past six months, she had been on secondment from the elite Serious Crimes Unit, to work on a project dealing with the asylum seekers who had flocked to the city in recent years.

Six months ago, a girl had been found by the river. She had been savagely beaten, then left to die. There was evidence of old brutality on her body, she was HIV positive, and had tuberculosis. She was probably from North Africa, probably in the country illegally. That was all they knew.

"We have to get a handle on these people," Tina's then boss, Roy Farnham said. He was speaking to the team who were dealing with the incident but his eyes had been on Tina. He was looking at a problem, and also at a solution. "Think you can handle this, Tina?"

The secondment was Farnham's offer to her. Get a line in there. Bring back something that will help us solve this kind of crime. She knew the subtext: *Clean up your act, get back on top of things. One chance, your only one.*

She checked her watch. She had to get to work. She scrabbled in her bag for her lipstick and eye pencil, and concentrated on putting her face together. She painted her mouth red and was brushing a line under her eye when her phone rang, making her hand slip. "Shit." She scrubbed at the smudge with a tissue as she groped in her bag for her phone. "Tina Barraclough."

"Tina." She recognised the voice. It was Dave West, her partner from her days with Farnham's unit. She and West had started on the job together, started the climb up the ladder together, but Dave was now a DS, with the possibility of promotion to DI on the horizon. Tina, who had been the promising recruit with the glittering prospects, had crashed and burned, and was beginning the slow climb again.

"Dave. Hi. How are you?"She hadn't seen him – hadn't seen any of them – for months. She was lying low.

"Fine. You? Enjoying the crossing patrols?"

"Yeah, yeah. And how's it going at Carnage Central?" She finished her other eye, her mouth distorted into the grimace that the application of mascara seemed to require. She may not have seen anyone on the team, but she couldn't stop herself from keeping tracks on what they were doing. Currently, they were involved in the long, ongoing and usually fruitless battle against proliferating drugs in the city.

"We've got someone in we're interviewing. Thing is, he claims to know you – looks like he's one of yours."

"One of mine?"

"Illegal immigrant. You know."

"Failed asylum seeker. Who is he?" Tina had met more people than she could remember in the past few months. She slipped her coat on, wrapping a scarf closely round her neck. It was cold out there.

"The name's Hamade, Amir Hamade. He won't

give us the time of day, but he says he'll talk to you." Paper rustled.

Tina was reaching for her car keys. Her hand stopped. Amir Hamade. He had been one of her main contacts within the asylum seekers' group, one of the few people who was prepared to give her a chance. He had been cautious with her, meticulously polite, but wary, very wary. He was in his thirties, a man who concealed the darkness of his past behind a gentle smile and impenetrable courtesy. "What's the problem?"

"He was picked up last night. A girl was strangled near Rutland Road."

"And you think Amir...?"

"We *know* he did it. A girl saw him before he ran away. His blood's at the scene, his prints are on her bag, a witness saw them together earlier that evening – said it looked as though they were arguing. Open and shut."

"We're talking about Amir Hamade? You're sure?" There had to be a mistake. The man she knew wasn't a killer.

"That's the name he gave, and that's the name on his ID."

"If it's open and shut, why do you need me?"

"You got a problem with it?"

"No. I just don't get why you need me to talk to him. With everything you've got."

"The boss wants more."

Roy Farnham. He was a good detective. If Farnham didn't think it was open and shut, then maybe… "OK. I'll come in. I'll have to clear it with…"

"The boss has talked to them. He wants you in now."

She sighed, not quite concealing her annoyance at the high-handed way Farnham was once again reorganising her life. "OK. See you soon."

As she left the block, she saw, like a flag calling her in, a pair of trainers hanging from an overhead wire, the sign, supposedly, of gangs marking their territory, though more likely the local kids messing around. Even so, she could feel the familiar buildup of adrenaline, a mix of tension and excitement. It was something she missed, something, in her newly sober state, she needed.

She edged her car out into the rush hour traffic. Amir Hamade. Her instinct – based on more than ten years' experience – told her that Amir was not a killer, but what she'd heard sounded bad. She didn't know all the details, and she was in danger of letting her opinion get in the way of hard fact.

The sun was starting to rise as she joined the stop-go shuffle. The sky was cloudless. Across the valley, the wall of Park Hill reflected the dawn light. A tram snaked down the hill and onto the high bridge across the road.

How well did she know Amir? Not that well. One afternoon, he and Tina had talked, and for the first and the only time, he had opened up to her. He told her about his childhood when he had seen his friends blown to pieces in the streets by Iraqi missiles during the long Iran/Iraq war, he'd seen his parents arrested and thrown in prison, an experience that had shortened his father's life. As an adult he'd spoken out against the execution of a teenage boy who had been publicly hanged, accusing the authorities of torture. He'd been beaten and tortured himself.

Men did not always come out of such experiences intact.

The traffic edged towards West Bar. Tina let the car creep forward, lane hopping to gain a car length when she saw an opportunity, cutting up a van as she moved back into the inside lane. The old Police HQ where she had started her time with the force looked derelict, the glass dirty and the concrete stained by the decades. This part of the city had missed the surge of renovation that recession had brought to a standstill.

She tapped her horn to galvanise a driver who was hesitating at the roundabout, then swung across the traffic and into position for the turning to the multi-storey. She was lucky there were no traffic patrols around. She was driving like an idiot, and she was doing it to keep her mind off Amir.

She had to drive almost to the top of the car park before she found a space. She stayed behind the wheel, her gaze fixed on the winter light sandwiched between the concrete blocks. There was no point trying to kid herself. She had been drawn to Amir from the time she first saw him. Despite his courtesy and the meticulous distance he kept between them, she had seen a returned interest in his face, and appreciation of her as a woman.

She would listen to what Amir had to say, and pass on what she found to the investigation team. That was her role here, nothing else.

The new Police HQ was a modern building of red brick and glass. When Tina had been seconded to the community policing unit, the HQ had been in the process of moving from the old 60s block, a massive and forbidding fortress, its cracked window panes and scruffy interior reflecting the role that many people thought the police played: the street cleaners, the people who swept up the dirt that society left behind. She was glad she didn't have to walk through the familiar door and along familiar corridors.

This was new territory to reflect new times.

She was directed to the incident room, where Farnham was completing the morning's briefing. He acknowledged her as she took an inconspicuous seat by the door. "Barraclough."

She busied herself with her notebook and pen, aware of curious glances. She ignored them and concentrated on the panels where photographs of the victim were displayed. The woman looked fragile and broken. One of her shoes, a flimsy party slipper, had fallen off. Her toe nails were painted, a colour that looked black in the lamp light. The paint was chipped.

The dead face looked deceptively peaceful apart from the trickle of blood from her mouth. This wasn't someone Tina had met. She tried to concentrate on what Farnham was saying.

"OK. To summarise. The victim is a Somali woman, Farah Jafari, 19. She's awaiting the result of an asylum claim. She had some accommodation, a room in a shared house, but the people who live there haven't seen her for a while. DC Barraclough, maybe you'd like to talk us through this a bit."

Tina felt the interest in the room shift in her direction. She stood up and moved to the front, realising the short skirt and Jimmy Choos were probably a mistake. She faced the team, registering the familiar faces, and the new ones, and wondering how many of them knew she had left the squad in disgrace, and what kind of disgrace it had been.

"OK. Asylum seekers. A woman like Farah Jafari will have had her claim assessed when she arrived here, then she will have been sent to whichever city they chose under the dispersal programme. She'll have been given some kind of accommodation and a small allowance, and then she'll have had to wait for her case to be heard." She looked at Farnham. "If she left the accommodation, she was in danger of losing it. If she fell out of the system she could lose her status as an asylum seeker. I don't get it."

"She'd got what she wanted. She'd got in." The speaker was someone Tina didn't know, a new recruit since her day. "Why do they come here? There's lots of places closer they could go. Somalia? It's on the other side of Africa. Why was she here in the first place? Didn't do her much good, did it?" He shrugged. "Just saying."

Dave West intervened. "I've had a call from Vice. They've seen this girl a couple of times down Shalesmoor." This was the area where street prostitutes currently operated. The previous speaker nodded as if his comment had been vindicated. "They tried to take her in, but she did a runner. They didn't know she was an illegal."

"She wasn't. That's the point." Tina was

depressed to hear her colleagues talking like this, but it didn't surprise her. "She'd be terrified of being arrested. That usually means they get sent to a detention centre." She looked at the man who had spoken. "It's not that simple..."

Farnham cut her off. "We're not here to debate the asylum laws. We're here because we've got a dead nineteen year old. One scenario we're considering in the light of what Vice says is that Hamade picks her up, they go down the alley to do business, something goes wrong. She ends up dead, he panics and runs. "West, I'd like you to finish off here." As he left the room, he caught Tina's eye. "Barraclough. My office. Five minutes."

She put her notes away, delaying on purpose. She wasn't sure what Farnham wanted. A sense of déjà vu settled round her as she walked along the corridor to his office.

"Sit down, Barraclough," Farnham said without ceremony as she came in. He might as well have seen her yesterday, not six months ago.

He studied her for a moment over steepled fingers. The last time she'd faced him like this, his voice had been mild, his message had been deadly: *You don't fuck witnesses, Barraclough, literally* or *metaphorically*. If he was remembering the same incident, he gave no sign. "So. Farah Jafari. What was she playing at?"

"Sir?"

"You've just told us she had a place, she had some money, she was safe for now. Why was she on the street? Why was she turning tricks?"

"I don't know. A Somali woman – it's not something she'd do willingly. She must have been desperate."

"OK." He made a note. "Keep your ear to the ground. Now. Amir Hamade. You know him?"

"Not very well. I've met him at Nadifa's House. He works as a volunteer."

"He's what? Claiming he's a political refugee?"

"Yes."

"But he's been refused."

"Yes. I think he's trying to make another claim, but... yes."

"OK. Did he have a bad time?"

"Apparently."

Farnham thought for a moment. "So, if he's telling the truth – he could be seriously disturbed."

Farnham's comments echoed her own thoughts. "Most asylum seekers – they're more likely to hurt themselves than someone else."

Farnham raised his eyebrows slightly.

"It's just – that's the statistics. That's all."

He waited, but Tina decided the hole was deep enough. It was time to stop digging.

When she didn't continue, he said, "The evidence points at Hamade. He says he met her on the way to this night shelter place and gave her his coat because she was cold. He says he went back to look for her – he's not saying why. For some reason, he decided to wander along the gennel and tripped over her corpse just around the time our witness nips down there for a pee. How does it sound to you?"

It sounded as though Amir was lying.

"It wasn't robbery," Farnham said. "She had £50 in her pocket, and she had her phone."

"£50? That's a hell of a lot for... How did she die?"

"She was strangled."

Close contact, hands round the neck of a struggling victim. Strangulation could happen when an attacker panicked, or it could be a slow, lethal enhancement of a perverted pleasure. "It doesn't sound like Amir Hamade to me, sir."

Farnham's gaze met hers. "I thought you didn't know him." It was about as loaded as a comment could be, and Tina was angry with herself as she felt her face flood with colour.

"I don't. Not well. He just doesn't seem the type. Sir."

"OK. Tell me what you do know about him – and this Nadifa's House thing. I need the background here."

So this was why Farnham had agreed to Amir's

request. Basically, he wanted to pick Tina dry, and this was the quickest way to do it.

***

Dave West was waiting for her outside the interview room. "The boss brief you?" he said.

"Yes. It's a straightforward interview. If he won't cooperate, then we log his refusal to talk. Is his lawyer...?"

"He doesn't want one."

Tina frowned. Amir was in deep shit. He needed legal advice and he needed it now. She was uneasy as she followed West into the interview room, closing the door behind her.

"Ma'am." Amir stood up, giving her the slight bow, his hand touching his chest, that was his mark of courtesy. She could see the relief on his face. He thought she was his friend. "Thank you for coming."

Farnham had made it clear she was here to conduct an interview, no more. She waited as West switched on the recording equipment and went through the preliminaries, introducing himself and Tina, and establishing for the record that Amir knew his rights to legal representation, and had turned this down. Amir listened quietly, responding with a yes or a no when required. She saw his face set into blankness as he realised that Tina was there for the police, not for him. She wanted to apologise to him, to explain, but she couldn't.

"Amir, do you understand why you are here?"

He bowed his head in assent. "I understand, ma'am."

"You've been arrested on suspicion of the murder of a young woman."

"I know, ma'am."

"I want you to tell me what happened. When did you first meet the woman?"

"I meet her on the street. She follow me."

"That was the first time you saw her?" She remembered West telling the team that both Amir and Jafari had been at Nadifa's House that afternoon.

"It was, ma'am." She had run into the barrier of Amir's unfailing politeness before. He would only tell her what he thought she wanted to hear, or, of course, what he wanted her to hear. She ran her options through her head, quickly.

"Were you at Nadifa's House yesterday afternoon?"

"I was, ma'am."

"But you didn't see the woman there?"

"I did not."

No explanation, no embellishment, just the minimal facts. "Amir, it's a very small place. We know she was there for at least 30 minutes. I find it hard to believe that you didn't…"

Again, he gave her that slight inclination of the head in acknowledgement. "I understand, ma'am. I was in the office for much of the time. I didn't see her."

Amir was a volunteer. It was possible he'd been in the office at the key time, and easy enough to check. "OK. So tell me when you first saw her."

Amir's story was straightforward, and hard to prove or disprove. He claimed he had met the girl on his way to the night shelter. She had asked him if he knew of anywhere she could stay the night, but the shelter didn't take women. When he got there, he'd felt bad about leaving her and had gone back to look for her. He studied his hands. "Then I find…"

"Why did you go down the gennel?"

He gave her a look of incomprehension.

"The alleyway."

"I think she might be sheltering there, ma'am."

Now she knew he was lying. He had asked for her because he thought she would believe him, but he had forgotten that she was a police officer, she had a role to fulfil, and she was pretty sure she was being manipulated here. She met his gaze. "Amir, I don't believe you. I think you saw her at Nadifa's House. I think she propositioned you. Suggested you had sex with her," she amended when he looked confused. She saw his eyes narrow as he studied her, as if he was reassessing what he was seeing.

Perhaps she needed to reassess as well. He was no innocent abroad. If his story was true, he had faced far harder interrogations than this. "The police think you went with her to have sex, and something went wrong. They don't think you meant to kill her, but you did, and the sooner you tell us what happened, the better."

He was shaking his head. "No. Ma'am, that's not true."

"Then tell me what really happened. Amir, you asked to talk to me. I came here because you asked me to. Don't treat me like a fool. Tell me the truth."

"I have told you…"

"No, Amir, you haven't. Stop playing games."

His gaze dropped to the table in front of him. She felt torn between the satisfaction of doing her job well, and guilt that she wasn't helping him the way he had wanted. She suppressed the guilt. He'd been lying to her. What did he expect?

"Ma'am, I can't tell you any more. I didn't kill her."

Half an hour later, Tina left the interview room with West. Amir had remained resolutely silent.

"Look, once we get the lab work through, we'll have him. We don't need a confession here," West consoled her.

"I know." The sound of Amir's voice, lying to her, squatted in her head. He had trusted her, but she was just another official, and he had had enough of those.

West stopped and looked down at her. "When are you coming back? You're needed. You're good at this. You know that."

She didn't know how to respond, so she said nothing.

***

Tina spent the next two hours at her desk, trying to work on her report, but she couldn't get the events of the morning out of her head. Amir's story had been... pathetic. It had been pathetic. He was an intelligent man, a resourceful one. He wouldn't have survived if he wasn't, so why hadn't he come up with a more convincing story?

The answer was there in front of her: because he was guilty. Why couldn't she accept that? Because she knew enough about Amir to know this was completely out of character? Or was there another reason, one that she couldn't admit to, and couldn't trust?

"Got a problem?"

Tina looked up. The CI in charge of the unit, Sara Hakim, was standing in front of her desk.

"Oh. No, sorry, ma'am. Daydreaming."

Hakim looked friendly enough. "Did everything go OK this morning?"

"Yes. Well, no, not really. Amir wouldn't tell me anything."

Hakim nodded, unsurprised. "OK. You did what you could. How's the report going?"

"I'll have it ready for next week." The following week was her deadline.

"Good. Then we need to talk about what you want to do next. Have you had any thoughts?"

Tina didn't want to discuss it, not yet. She had a question to ask. "I was wondering... A devout Muslim wouldn't use a prostitute, right?"

"Well, on paper. Same as devout Christians, Hindus, you name it. People don't always do what they're supposed to do."

"It seems out of character for Amir, that's all."

"Maybe she propositioned him, and he saw a Muslim woman breaking the rules. Something like that could trigger a violent response."

Her problem was that she was thinking like a

Westerner. She was a pragmatist, she had no religious beliefs and she wasn't aware of anyone on Farnham's team who had. Maybe some of them were church on Sundays sort of believers, but...

Amir *was* devout. His faith was his life. He wouldn't have had to escape from his country if he had been prepared to compromise on his beliefs.

And his beliefs wouldn't allow him to lie, not about something as important as this. Perhaps his story was so weak because he had told her the truth, but only part of it. It was what he hadn't told her that would give Farnham's team the information they needed, and for some reason Amir wasn't talking.

Ma'am, I can't tell you any more. I didn't kill her.

I didn't kill her. He wouldn't have said that if it wasn't true. He would have said nothing. She picked up her phone, then put it down again. It wasn't her case. It wasn't her investigation. It wasn't her team. Her hunches were irrelevant.

Except... Farnham wasn't convinced by the case against Amir either.

She saved what she'd written and closed the file. It was after one. Working here meant regular breaks, lunch, coffee, home at five. She still hadn't got used to it so she rarely took the time, but today, she had something she wanted to do.

"Going for lunch?"one of the other women asked as she stood up from her desk. "I'll join you."

"No. I've got to go to St Barnabas's. I need some information."

It was starting to rain. The thought of spending half an hour over a sandwich reading a magazine in a local cafe was compelling, but instead she headed for her car.

The night shelter was a fifteen minute drive from the city centre, but a long walk for people who had to get there without any access to transport. It was located in one of the poorer areas of the city, one that had been wealthy enough once, with streets of decaying Victorian houses where high trees cast their shadows across the roads.

Tina parked down the road from the church, by a small green space enclosed behind metal railings, the grass overgrown, the branches of trees hanging heavily down. She could see the church steeple dominating the sky.

The shelter was based further down the hill, a small, low building that had once been the church hall in the days when St Barnabas's had an active congregation. She walked towards the church, her feet complaining about her new shoes.

She should have called ahead. There was no guarantee that anyone would be here, but as it turned out, she was in luck. There was a light on inside and the heavy wooden door stood ajar. She went in.

Her first breath took her back to her childhood, to Sundays standing next to her mother in the rows of pews, listening as the words of the service floated above her head. Tina had been a devout child, a trait that had followed her into her teenage years, and then dissipated with the heady discovery of sex.

The central aisle lay in front of her, illuminated by a dim light that made its way through the screens protecting the windows. Between the pillars, the space vanished into the shadows. There were no pews, and her footsteps echoed. She walked slowly down the aisle towards a small table that was set out to face the congregation. Behind it, a traditional altar stood, swathed in drapes, dusty and unused. There was no transept, just a rail between the nave and the sanctuary.

She looked up at the high roof, turning as she did so, and almost walked into a woman who had approached her silently from the back of the church. "Shit!" The expletive jumped out before she could stop it.

The woman frowned as she looked at Tina. "Can I help you?"

"Sorry. You made me jump." Tina showed her ID card. "I'm DC Tina Barraclough. I'm with the SYP liaison unit. I wanted to talk to..." She racked her memory. "to the minister, Mr Radcliffe." She was studying the woman, and realised she was under the same scrutiny herself.

"I'm Karen Morgan. Is it important? Mr Radcliffe is very busy." The woman's mouth closed in a thin line. Her face looked tense, almost angry, with deep furrows between the brows.

"I wanted to ask him about last night. You know a woman was killed near Rutland Road..."

Her eyebrows rose in an exaggerated arc of surprise. "That's hardly liaison unit business."

Tina wondered what had triggered this hostility. The expletive, presumably. She made her smile friendly. "But it involves the community. Things like this can have repercussions. We need to know what's been happening." She noticed that Karen Morgan was wearing a blue suit that was almost a uniform. She must have some formal role here. A deaconess?

Morgan's expression didn't change. "The police have already been. I'm sure they'll be

41

happy to pass on any information you need. Now if you'll excuse..."

"Miss Morgan, I am the police and I need some more information. Is Mr Radcliffe here?"

"He's very busy. What do you want to know?" Her eyes took in Tina from the scarlet lipstick to the red shoes.

"Were you at the shelter last night?"

"Of course not. No women. You're supposed to know that."

Tina stepped hard on her temper. "Then I need to speak to Mr Radcliffe."

"He wasn't there when it happened. Not that it happened at the shelter."

"I wasn't there when what...? Oh, I see. It's OK, Karen. I can deal with this."

An expression of resentment flashed across Karen Morgan's face. The man walking down the aisle towards them didn't look much like the ministers Tina remembered from her childhood. He was young – about her age – and wearing jeans and a t-shirt. He was tall, with the solid, muscular build of a sportsman, a rugby player, maybe.

"I'm sorry you've been disturbed," Karen Morgan said to him. Her face had softened, suddenly looking much younger.

"That's OK, Karen. I've just about finished." He looked at Tina. "I'm Jim Radcliffe. And you are...?"

"She says she's from the SYP liaison." Karen Morgan looked angry again. Suddenly, Tina understood what the problem was. No attractive woman was going to be a welcome visitor for Radcliffe, in Morgan's eyes. She'd staked her claim. *Keep off, sister.*

Karen Morgan's hostility tempted her to flirt with Radcliffe who looked as if he might enjoy such an exchange. *Professional*, she reminded herself. "DC Barraclough." She showed him her identification.

His glance seemed cursory, but she got the impression he'd taken in enough to ensure she was the genuine article. He looked at her with interest. "The liaison unit? I'm surprised we haven't met before."

"I've been working with Nadifa's House."

His face lit up. "I know them well. How can I help you?"

Karen Morgan's lips thinned. Tina included them both in her response. "I'm here because of Amir Hamade."

"The liaison team are investigating the murder?"

"No. But I wanted to know what happened at the shelter last night – I want to be as informed as possible. There'll be bad feeling, Amir being arrested." It sounded thin to her. Behind Radcliffe, Karen Morgan raised her eyebrows in silent comment.

"You'd better come into the office, DC Barraclough." Without waiting to see if she was following, he led the way down the aisle to a small door to the right of the altar, behind the lectern. Karen hurried after him

Through the door, the church architecture became 60's dingy. She followed them along a corridor past doors marked 'store' and 'basement' to a small office. He looked round the room distractedly, running a hand through his hair. Two upholstered chairs faced each other in a corner. His face brightened and he gestured her into one of them, then waited until Karen, after a brief hesitation, sat down in the other.

The room was in need of a coat of paint. Papers were scattered across the desk, and typed sheets were pinned up on the wall above it. Tina scanned them: *Night Shelter Dates, Rota, Volunteers' Contact Details.*

An umbrella stand containing a couple of rather battered umbrellas and, incongruously, a cricket bat, had been pulled against the door to keep it open. Radcliffe saw her glance at it and smiled. "I used to play. Souvenirs of a past life. Do you want coffee?" There was a kettle on the floor and some mugs and a bottle of milk on the windowsill.

"Please."

Radcliffe glanced at Karen, who gave her head an angry shake, then he switched on the kettle and spooned coffee powder into two mugs. "Sugar?"

"No thanks. I'll have mine black," she added as she saw him sniff the milk with a dubious expression on his face.

"Wise choice." He grinned as he passed her a mug full of hot black liquid. He leaned against the edge of the desk. "OK, go ahead. I'll tell you what I know." He frowned. "Amir? Do you really think...?"

"I'm not on the case. I don't know. You were here last night?"

He nodded. "I'd like to be here every night, but it isn't possible. We have a good team of volunteers."

"But you weren't here until after 11," Karen said. "Were you?" She looked at Tina, not quite meeting her eyes. "I know because I dropped him off. He wasn't here when Amir Hamade came."

"My car's out of action," he said. "But I was here after that."

"You've already.... Oh, never mind." Karen hunched herself crossly in her chair.

"Who else was on duty?

"Andre Mutombo. He's a refugee from DRC. He does a lot of work for Nadifa's House."

Tina glanced at the rota on the wall. The name of Andre Mutombo was there, along with his address and phone number. "He was here all night?"

"He opened the place up. Then I took over. By then, there were..." He counted on his fingers. "...twelve visitors."

"All men?"

"We don't offer accommodation to women." Before Tina could ask, he said, "We can't offer segregated accommodation, and there's almost nothing else available for the men."

"How well did you know Farah Jafari?"

He was frowning slightly as he answered. "She came to the advice centre. We always keep an eye on the young ones. DC Barraclough, I thought you weren't investigating..."

"We've already answered all these questions. This is a waste of your time." Karen Morgan spoke to Radcliffe, ignoring Tina.

"I must admit..." he began.

"I'm sorry. I'm just trying to get a picture of what happened last night."

"Well, according to Andre Mutombo, Amir arrived, asked if he could leave his bag and went back to look for someone. He said he was coming back."

"With Farah Jafari? He said that?"

"I don't think so. As I said, we have no accommodation for women. And before you ask, yes, I follow the rules to the letter. If we want the shelter to continue, we have to stick to our agreement."

"Do you know why Farah went to Nadifa's House that day?"

He shook his head. "She asked to speak to an advisor, but she left before anyone was free."

"I'm trying to work out why she was on the street."

"I don't know. I don't understand it. She had somewhere to live. She had a reasonable case. I didn't know there was a problem until we got the news. I understand now she hadn't been at her accommodation for a couple of weeks."

"Maybe something scared her?"

Karen Morgan spoke up suddenly. "She was scared of being put in detention. The police thought she was soliciting."

"Soliciting?" Radcliffe looked shocked. "Where did you hear that?"

"From the police. When they interviewed me. Did I know Farah Jafari was a prostitute? I told them I knew no such thing."

Radcliffe looked from Karen to Tina. "Is that true?"

"She was seen on the street around Shalesmoor. It's possible. They tried to talk to her, but she ran away."

Radcliffe's expression hardened. "She was a child. Her papers said she was nineteen, but I doubt she was more than seventeen. She needed protection, not hassle."

There was nothing Tina could say. The Vice Squad had their job to do. She had no control of that. "There's just..."

"Look, DC Barraclough, I've given you as much time as I can. If police action drove Farah away from her home, it left a vulnerable young woman on the street. And now she's been murdered. If you'll excuse me, I have things to do."

We're not social workers, Tina wanted to say, but he knew that. "Thank you for your time."

Karen Morgan saw her off the premises. She didn't speak. Routed, Tina returned to the car. She wondered how much truth there was in Radcliffe's accusation. Farah Jafari had run away from the police when they'd tried to pick her up. It was true that if she'd been charged, she might well have ended up in detention. The asylum seekers were terrified of the detention centres with their casual racism and their abuse.

She'd found out one thing that Amir hadn't told her. He'd spoken to a volunteer, Andre Mutombo, that night. As she'd left the office, she'd memorised Mutombo's contact details from the notice on the wall.

She wasn't sure what to do now. Mutombo was the only person who had seen Amir at the crucial time. She wanted to hear what he had to say, but talking to him was outside anything she could legitimately pretend was part of her current project.

She tapped her fingers against the steering wheel, thinking. Her report had to be finished by the end of the week. Whatever plans she had when this assignment was over, she couldn't afford to fuck up again. *Leave it, Tina.* She advised herself. *Forget it.*

But she had never been good at taking advice.

***

Andre Mutombo lived in an old 60's development near the city centre. Dual carriageways ran past two sides, and uneven pathways led into the maze of the estate. Concrete blocks rose vertically around Tina as she picked her way along the path that was strewn with fast food cartons, drinks cans, sweet wrappers, the detritus of the people who passed through.

The estate was a labyrinth. She looked round, trying to get her bearings. Stairways seemed to run into the blocks at random. She could see groups of teenagers on the walkways, looking down at her, a white intruder into territory that wasn't hers.

She went under an arch between two apartment blocks and found herself in an open space where a group of children were kicking a ball around in the fading light. Andre Mutombo lived at number 38. She found the flat more by luck than judgement, then knocked on the door.

Footsteps approached. She waited a moment, then knocked again. "Mr Mutombo? It's Detective Constable Barraclough from South Yorkshire Police. Could I talk to you for a minute?"

The door opened. The man on the other side seemed to fill the entrance. His head was shaven, but he had a heavy beard. "I am Andre Mutombo. How may I help you?" The words were carefully polite, but she could see another emotion underlying them – hostility? Suspicion? She wasn't sure. She was suddenly aware that she'd come here with scant authority, and no backup.

"Mr Mutombo. I wanted to ask you about what happened last night when Amir Hamade came to the night shelter."

It was definitely hostility. She fought an impulse to step back. "I have already talked to the police. What else do you want to know?"

"I'm sorry. I just need to confirm some details my colleague…" She could feel a nervous smile starting to stretch her face. *Fuck's sake, Tina. Get a grip.*

"Details?"

"Can you confirm the time that Amir Hamade arrived at the shelter?"

His eyes were cold. "As I said, just after 11."

"And what happened then?"

"He asked if he could leave his bag and go find someone."

"Who?"

"I don't know."

"Didn't he say?"

"No."

"He says he went to look for a woman who asked him for help."

"Maybe. I don't recall."

"You don't remember much."

He shrugged. "It was just another night."

"What did he plan to do? If he found her?"

He shrugged again.

"Was he going to bring her back to the shelter?"

"No women there. Men only."

She was getting impatient with his stonewalling. "I didn't ask you about the rules. I asked you if Amir was planning to bring her back."

"Maybe you should ask the woman. She is the one who chases the men."

"Farah Jafari is dead, Mr Mutombo, so I'm asking you. Did you know her?"

"I did not." He held her gaze, his hostility almost palpable. He was about to say something else, when feet clattered on the walkway behind her, and a small boy in a red and white striped shirt appeared, one of the footballers. "Dad, I got..."

Mutombo spoke to the child in French, a fast, accented French that Tina could barely understand.

The child's face crumpled in indignant protest, then seeing his father's expression, he came to the door.

"You support United?" she said to him as he passed her, pointing at his shirt.

He looked at her doubtfully. Mutombo spoke again, more sharply this time, and the child vanished inside. "Is that everything?"

"Was Amir planning to bring the woman back to the shelter?"

"Ask him. I don't know. Now, I've got things I have to do."

He was about the close the door on her. "Mr Mutombo, what's your immigration status?" She didn't like herself for using this weapon, but he'd rubbed her up the wrong way. If his case was still being decided, or if he had been refused and was trying for an appeal, he wouldn't want to get on the wrong side of the authorities. He was hiding something and she wanted to know what it was.

His eyes narrowed. "Listen, Miss. I have two children. I have leave to remain, you know what that means? I get to stay, for now. I don't get to work, I don't get to support my kids, I get to live on handouts and I get to take shit from the immigration. I don't get to take shit from you."

The door shut in her face.

As she emerged from the stairway, she saw the children were still playing in the twilight. She stood and watched the game. When the ball came in her direction, she stopped it with her foot, and waited until one of the boys came to retrieve it. "The lad in the United strip – is he Mutombo?"

The boy looked at her warily. "Dunno." He kicked the ball back into the game.

"Who else lives in that flat?"

The boy glanced up. Tina's gaze followed his, and she saw Andre Mutombo watching them from the walkway. Before she could move, the football came from nowhere and smacked her on the side of the head. She staggered and tripped, feeling her heel turn in the soft earth. She sat down heavily, catching herself with her hands which stung as they hit the ground.

The children laughed. It wasn't a friendly

sound. "She drunk!" one of them shouted, and the jeer was taken up as Tina scrambled to her feet. She brushed off the dirt and assessed the damage. Her stockings were ruined, her elbow was bruised, and the heel of her shoe had snapped.

When she looked back up to the walkway, Mutombo had gone.

She limped back to her car where someone had written *cunt* in the dirt on the bonnet. She sat in the driver's seat and inspected her broken shoe. It looked beyond repair.

What had she found out? Mutombo was supporting his children. There was no sign of a wife or mother to help him. He was a young man, or young enough, and he looked like an angry one. What did he do to satisfy his sexual needs?

She knew there was something – something she had heard, or seen, or thought about, something that she needed to follow up. She ought to go to Farnham, or talk it over with Dave, but she wasn't sure there was anything useful she could tell them. *Please, sir, Amir Hamade didn't kill Farah Jafari because he doesn't tell lies.* Yeah, right. Good move, Tina.

Time to go.

As she put the car in gear, she realised she was just 100 metres away from a petrol station. She hesitated for a moment, causing the car behind her to sound its horn. She flicked a finger at the driver and pulled into the forecourt. She went in and bought a packet of 20 Bensons.

***

The next morning, Tina found herself in Sara Hakim's office within minutes of walking through the door. "What the hell are you playing at, Tina? I had a complaint from St Barnabas's. Apparently you walked in and questioned James Radcliffe about the murder."

"A complaint? Why?" Her ankle was sore from her fall yesterday.

"And gossiping about a case – that you are barely involved in. Is that your idea of professional behaviour?"

"Ma'am, with respect, it wasn't gossip. There's a connection. Hamade's well known and well-liked."

"So you went and questioned James Radcliffe?"

"I asked him about what happened that night, yes. I didn't question him." She wondered if she should express her doubts about Amir's guilt, but she had nothing to back up her hunch, or nothing concrete. A feeling... That wasn't enough.

Hakim frowned. "Tina, we depend on the good will of Nadifa's House, and people like James Radcliffe. They give us the access we get to the community. We can't ignore law breaking – we don't. But within those limits, we have established a good relationship. When a member of my team starts interrogating the people we've been working with, it undoes months of work."

From the point of view of the liaison work, she had abused Radcliffe's trust. Thank God Hakim didn't know about Andre Mutombo. "I'm sorry, ma'am. It won't happen again."

"OK, Tina, I'm prepared to leave it there. Just remember, you need to focus on your own responsibilities, not someone else's. Is that report going to be finished in time?"

"Yes, ma'am."

She went back to her desk and opened up the files containing her report, and wearily scrolled down to the paragraph she had been working on the night before, the section on crime levels within the group. She began to read, to remind herself where she was.

Petty crime in the asylum seeker community is rare. An analysis of crime figures from the South Yorkshire area shows that recorded offences within this group relate mainly to illegal employment....

Remorselessly, her mind went back to the killing. The £50 worried her. It was unlikely Farah Jafari would have turned up at Nadifa's House if she had £50 in her pocket, or if she'd felt able to earn £50. Had she stolen it, and if so, who had she stolen from? Jafari had gone to Nadifa's House for help, but she had done a runner before they could do anything for her. Why?

She had been destitute, possibly keeping herself alive by casual prostitution. Again, why? Until her case was heard and refused, she had a right to accommodation and a small amount of money. She was safe. It made no sense that she had been on the streets and desperate.

Her phone rang. It was Dave West. "Hi Dave. I was just thinking about you."

"Now she tells me. Did you call me 'Sir'?"

"Sir? Oh, hey, you got your promotion!"

"I got through the board. There's an inspector's job coming up on this team. Farnham wants me to go for it."

"That's brilliant." And she was pleased for him. But where was she? Still struggling on the lower grades, still getting bollockings from her boss.

"Yeah. It's time. Listen, you want to help me celebrate? We're meeting in The Bath Hotel." The white-tiled pub down a gennel near the city centre had always been a popular meeting place for them.

"What time?"

"Eight, eight-thirty."

"OK. Listen, before you go, is there any news about Amir Hamade?"

"Hamade? What's the big deal about Hamade?"

"Is there something new?"

"Look, Tina, you know I can't..."

"Come on, Dave. You're not a DI yet."

"If you paid me for all the shit you've got me into..."

"I know, but you still love me."

"OK, OK. The money Jafari had on her probably came from Nadifa's House. One of their workers had her purse stolen that afternoon. And we found Jafari's phone. Someone had stuck it in a crack in the wall, just behind the body. We nearly missed it."

"And?"

"And it had two calls on it that evening. Both of them from Hamade. It had his prints on as well."

He'd handled Jafari's phone – presumably when he hid it. "What about her other contacts?"

"Not many, all anonymous."

Most of her contacts would have been fellow

asylum seekers. Their phones were usually anonymous, phones they picked up second hand and topped up when they could, unregistered and unrecorded. "Clients?"

"No one with a traceable phone. The boss has got it plugged in, see if anyone calls, but it's a long shot."

Those calls meant Amir had lied from start to finish. He had called Jafari, possibly arranged their meeting, and then... He knew how damning those calls were. That was why he'd hidden her phone. Her belief in his innocence was shaken, but she was still not convinced. Something was wrong.

***

Tina went back to her flat. She wasn't meeting Dave until eight. She made herself some toast, then discarded it half-eaten. She wasn't hungry. Restlessness made her pace the flat: living room, kitchen, bedroom, up and down.

She showered and washed her hair, then went back into the bedroom to rummage through her wardrobe. She inspected her shoes, but the heel had snapped clean off. They were irreparable. Serve her right for sticking her nose in where it wasn't wanted.

She was putting off getting ready. She couldn't find the energy to be sociable. She could remember the nights when she danced until daylight, fell into bed, either alone or in company, and was up the next day and ready for work, her mind in overdrive, the energy and enthusiasm fizzing through her veins. Tina Barraclough, marked for great things.

And then there had been the days when she'd had to drag herself out of bed, take something – anything – to give her enough momentum to crawl into work, days when the job was the only thing in her life that she wanted, but the thing in her life she hated the most.

It had started to go wrong in the aftermath of a bad case. A young man had fallen to his death from a tower block, landing almost at her feet. She could still see the smashed wreck of his body on the ground in front of her, his blood spattered across her clothes.

Most of the people she'd worked with then had moved on, but they'd all been affected by that case. Dave was the only one she still saw, and his happy-go-lucky approach to the job had changed that night. He became serious, and he became ambitious. And Tina? She had changed too.

She picked up her phone and texted Dave: *Sorry got 2 work another time ok inspector luv t xxx.*

The packet of cigarettes she had bought was

in her bag, still unopened. She took it out and peeled the cellophane off. SMOKING CAN KILL!

You don't say.

She took the photograph of Farah Jafari out of her bag. Nineteen. Farah Jafari had been nineteen. She left the chaos of Somalia and came to the UK because someone had promised her safety. She had come here for sanctuary, and she had found violence and death. Tina was supposed to do something about things like this.

She opened a bottle of wine and poured herself a large glass, her first drink in weeks. She put the open packet of cigarettes and her lighter on the desk beside her and started work.

She sat up that night working on her report, finishing everything she should have been doing while she was chasing around after Amir and Farah Jafari.

By six in the morning, she was finished. The glass of wine was untouched beside her, and the cigarettes were still in their packet. She poured the wine away, threw the cigarettes into the kitchen bin, then went and stood under the shower, turning the control round to cold, until she was halfway to alertness.

She heated up last night's coffee in the microwave, but she couldn't face breakfast. She stood in front of the mirror, and put on her makeup. The face that looked back at her was pale and drawn.

***

Like all big organisations, South Yorkshire Police suffered from gaps in internal communication. There were times when the left hand not only didn't know what the right hand was doing, it didn't even seem aware that the right hand existed. Tina was banking on this gap today.

The first thing she did was to call Nadifa's House. "I'm calling from St Barnabas," she said. "Can I just check the rota? Is Andre at the shelter tonight?"

He was.

Andre Mutombo knew more than he had told her, and she wanted to find out what it was. He'd been at the shelter when Amir had arrived that evening – she wanted to hear his account of the events of that night herself. The problem was, she'd alienated him with her last visit. His hostility had unnerved her, she'd been impatient, and she'd made a stupid mistake. OK. First thing to do was apologise, the second thing to do was get him to understand she wasn't working with the investigating team, she was trying to help Amir.

It would be a calculated risk going back to St Barnabas.

Left hand, right hand.

Would she get away with it? Mutombo was the key to this case, she was sure of it.

***

It was after ten-thirty when Tina drove out of the city centre. The streets were empty. There were few cars on the dual carriageway that led out of the city, just the relentless rumble of lorries heading west to Manchester, to Liverpool, the great cities of the industrial age.

She turned off the main road up the hill past the gennel where Farah Jafari had died. The railway viaduct loomed above her, then she was at the top of the hill and into the narrow back streets where red brick terraces lined the road.

The factory owners had built row upon row of these houses for their workers. The factories had gone, but the terraces still stood in ranks, lining the valley sides, the rows broken occasionally by lines of shops: insurance brokers, oriental grocers, budget supermarkets, villages in the middle of the urban sprawl.

It was quiet. Ice gleamed on the pavements. An owl hooted somewhere in the night, and then it was silent again. In the far distance,

Tina could hear the hum of traffic, but here, there was nothing.

The low building by the church, the place where the night shelter was located, was in darkness. She checked her watch. It was almost 11. The doors should be opening soon. As she got out of the car, she could see a dim light outlining one of the windows. Behind her, the church spire rose into the night, and the full moon turned the car park into a pool of grey and silver.

As she walked towards the entrance, she expected to see people approaching, people coming to the shelter for protection from the fierce cold of the winter night, but there was no one.

She tried the handle on the front door. It turned, and the door swung quietly open. She was in a small lobby where a notice, yellowed with curling edges, welcomed her to St Barnabas Church Hall. She went on through the doors facing her, and found herself in a dark corridor that smelled of dust and emptiness.

"Hello?"

Nothing.

She went along the corridor. An open door on her right led into a large, empty room. The floor was carpeted, and chairs were pushed back against the wall. There was a pile of bedding on a table under the window. A plug-in radiator leaked warmth into the air. This was where the homeless men could sleep away from the rigours of the weather and the dangers of the night streets.

Someone was expecting them. Someone had turned on the heater. She left the room and went further down the corridor. There was a small kitchen, and beyond that, an office. The office door was open, but the light was off and the room was empty.

"Hello? Mr Mutombo?"

Silence.

She went into the office and looked round. Again, there was evidence of recent activity. Papers were spread out on the desk. Someone had been in here, working. Her eyes scanned the walls, taking in the list of volunteers, the addresses and phone numbers, like the one in Radcliffe's office at the church, except it was covered with scrawled amendments.

Many of the volunteers were failed asylum seekers, and their phone numbers and addresses changed constantly. The exception was Andre Mutombo. His address was neatly typed, the one she had visited the day before. His phone number had been crossed out, and a new one written in.

She tried the desk drawers, but they were locked. Her gaze moved to the filing cabinet. She tried the top drawer, and it slid open smoothly. It was packed with ring-binders, all with hand-written labels on the spines: Events, AGM, Accounts – the records of the running of the church hall. Towards the back, she found one marked Night Shelter. She pulled it out.

She knew she was snooping, she had no right to look at this, but all her instincts were telling her to check, and to keep checking. She glanced over her shoulder, and lifted the folder out of the drawer. She put it on the desk and started turning the pages.

The shelter had been running for less than a year, and the binder was only half full. There were the names and contact details of asylum seekers who were working as volunteers for the shelter, the same list as the one of the wall, but without the crossings out and amendments. No one had updated this list.

There were minutes of meetings – she scanned them, seeing familiar names from Nadifa's House, the names of Jim Radcliffe and Karen Morgan, Andre Mutombo again had been a major participant, attending all the meetings as far as she could see, his name highlighted against several items marked for action.

Something was nagging at her mind, something in the records that she had seen, a connection...

She flicked through the pages again. There was a list of users of the shelter against dates that showed they had been helping between 10 and 15 men each night. And then... no one.

Since the murder, the users had stayed away.

These were the ones who made it to the UK. They were the survivors. They had an instinct for danger.

But she didn't. Not any more.

"What's going... DC Barraclough! What are you doing here?"

The voice spoke from behind her. She spun round, her heart hammering. Jim Radcliffe was standing in the doorway of the office, his height and his breadth filling it.

It took her a moment to catch her breath. "I came to see Andre Mutombo. The door was open."

He took the folder. "You have no right to look at these. You shouldn't be here. Andre? Andre doesn't want to talk to you."

So Radcliffe knew about her visit to Mutombo. She was probably in deep shit, but just now, she couldn't worry about that.

"Where is he?"

"He probably saw you pull up outside. He

won't come back while you're here."

"I was out of order with him. I wanted to apologise. I need to talk to him. I think he knows something about the night of the murder."

His eyes met hers. "Something that might help Amir?"

She shook her head. "I don't know."

"Surely they don't have enough to charge him."

"They do. I don't understand why they haven't. He isn't helping himself. He's lying and they know that."

Radcliffe's gaze was fixed on the folder, but she got the impression he wasn't seeing it. He seemed tense and uncertain, as if he was trying to come to a decision. "DC Barraclough, you're willing to break the rules if necessary, aren't you?"

"Are you going to put in another complaint?"

"That's not... I'm sorry about that. I'll... Listen, I need to know. It's important. You break rules if you have to, right?"

"Sometimes." What was this?

"I need to talk to you off the record. There's information the investigating team doesn't have. They need it."

"And you want me to take it to them?"

"Yes. I want you to guarantee you won't tell them where this came from."

"I can't guarantee that. Not without knowing what it is." She slipped her hand into her pocket and pressed the *record* button on her phone. "I'll listen."

He looked at her for what felt like a long time, then he nodded. "OK. Six months ago, a woman, no, a young girl, came to... someone... for help. You're following me? She was destitute and she was terrified. She told this person she'd escaped from the people who'd brought her here. She'd come to Sheffield with her friend, and now her friend had run away."

"A boyfriend?"

"No, another girl."

"Why didn't..." she could play along if she had to. "...this person tell her to go to the police? He could have gone with her."

"She'd been brought into the country illegally. She'd been held in a brothel, forced into prostitution. You know what would happen to her. The authorities would let her stay if she could identify the people who brought her in, but only for as long as it took to make a case. Either way, they'd send her back. If she gave evidence against the traffickers, her whole family could be in trouble. If she was sent back, where could she go? An ex-prostitute, possibly HIV positive by now? She'd have been dead within a year."

Instead, she was dead within six months.

"How does this affect the case against Amir?"

"Don't you see? The traffickers were after her. They'd already taken her friend back. A few weeks later, she's killed. Does that sound like coincidence to you?"

Traffickers. Six months ago, around the time Farah Jafari had come to Radcliffe, the body of an unknown woman had been found in the river. She had been beaten to death. "Why didn't you tell the police? It doesn't matter to her now."

"Think, Tina! I gave her shelter. I gave her money. I didn't say anything when she turned up with an ID card and papers I knew were fakes. How could I tell the police that?"

He'd covered up a crime. What he'd told her was close to an admission.

"What happened?" However hard her life may have been, she'd been coping. She had some kind of status and a place to live. But when she died, she had been destitute.

"She ran away. Maybe the traffickers caught up with her. That's why I'm telling you. Amir had no reason to kill her. The traffickers did."

"Not really. She was worth more to them alive. And Amir is lying. He made two phone calls to her that evening, but he says he didn't know her."

It was there again, that sense of something

she'd missed.

Radcliffe's phone rang. "Hello? Yes, I'm here... What?... Sorry, there was someone... No, nothing... I'm on my way."

He looked at Tina. "I need to get back to the church to lock up. I was only supposed to be a couple of minutes. Karen's holding the fort, but she needs to get home. I'm not running away. I'll be back. Ten minutes, OK?"

She wanted time to think. She wanted time to decide. She had recorded Radcliffe's story – the question was whether she needed to use it. "I'll wait."

She sat at the desk and keyed Dave West's number into her phone. Radcliffe had left the folder on the desk. She turned the pages idly as she waited for Dave to pick up.

"Tina. Changed your mind?" She could hear the noise around him, and the slur in his voice. She'd forgotten about his celebration.

"No. I'm at the Night Shelter. I've got important information about Farah Jafari. It's complicated. It's..."

"What?" The noise in the background burst into a chorus: *Why was he born so beautiful...* "Shut up. I can't hear..."

"The Night Shelter. Dave, it's important. I..." Her phone beeped. Low battery. She'd used up the charge recording Radcliffe's story. "My phone's running out of charge. I'll call you on the landline, right?"

She cut the call off and picked up the receiver of the desk phone, watching as the light went out on her mobile. Too late, she realised Dave's number was stored there. She couldn't remember it because she'd never dialled it. She just scrolled down to *Dave*, and pressed the key. She stared at the dead mobile in frustration. The information she wanted was in there, and she couldn't access it.

There were contact lists in the file. It was possible Sara Hakim's number was in there. Hakim could link her across to Farnham's team. She flicked through the pages. There was only the number for the Community Liaison office which would be closed by now. She'd have to wait until Radcliffe came back, then go into town. Radcliffe could take his story – he could tell it any way he wanted – to Farnham's team.

In the meantime, Andre Mutombo's number was here in the folder. He probably wasn't far away. If she could persuade him she was no threat, he might come back and talk to her. She keyed the number into the land line and waited. She could hear it ringing. At least he hadn't switched off.

After three rings, it was picked up. No one said anything. "Andre? Mr Mutombo? It's Tina

Barraclough. I know you don't want to talk to me, but..."

"Barraclough? What the fuck are you playing at?"

She was speaking to Roy Farnham.

"Sir, I'm at the Night Shelter. What are you..." The phone cut out.

Tina stared at it, and jiggled the receiver cradle. Nothing. The line was dead. The phone must have pulled loose. She followed the line round the wall, the receiver held to her ear. There was a clatter as the phone fell off the desk onto the floor.

The phone jack was still in the socket but the line was dead.

The significance of what she'd found was just beginning to dawn on her. The phone they'd found at the scene, the one Amir had hidden in a space in the wall, was connected in the incident room, waiting for someone to call it.

And someone had.

She looked at the rota on the wall. The number she'd dialled for Andre Mutombo had been scribbled out and a new one written in, but the list in the folder hadn't been updated.

It wasn't Amir propositioning Jafari, it was Andre Mutombo, his huge frame dwarfing her bruised fragility. It was his hands that closed round her neck, either in rage, or in a fulfilment of perverted lust, and in that moment, his phone slipped out of his pocket and onto the ground.

She saw Amir walking the streets, looking for the missing girl. She saw him keying Mutombo's number into his phone, calling him to ask if the shelter was still open.

And the phone had rung from the hidden gennel.

That was why Amir had not told them the truth. Andre Mutombo was his friend. He had children. If he was arrested, his children would be put into care, and if he was sent to jail, they would remain in the care system and be deported with their father once he was released.

She forced herself to think. Mutombo had been here, and not long ago. If he was the killer, then he was dangerous. She was alone here in the night shelter. Jim Radcliffe was somewhere on the empty street. She needed backup, now.

Then all her senses came alert. There was someone in the corridor.

"Jim?"

There was no reply. She grabbed her mobile and pressed the button. Sometimes the batteries picked up after the phone had been switched off. Her fingers were clumsy with haste. She saw the screen light up, *yes, yes, come on!* and the footsteps, the footsteps... Too close.

A hand reached past her and enclosed her wrist, giving it a sharp shake so that the phone dropped onto the floor with a clatter. Andre Mutombo was looking down at her, his face set, his eyes full of anger.

Tina twisted in his grasp, the toe of her shoe hacking into his shin. She knew how painful that was, she knew it could disable an attacker for a few vital seconds, but his grip didn't loosen. He pushed her away against the wall and kicked her phone beyond reach. The only sign that she had hurt him was the quickness of his breathing. "I won't let you do this," he said.

"You're too late. They know." Her voice sounded odd, as though she couldn't breathe, as though his fingers were already round her throat squeezing the life out of her, as they had squeezed the life out of Farah Jafari.

"They know what? That I'm a killer? That I'm going to prison and my sons will be abandoned? You don't know anything."

Tina's back was against the wall. The door was the only way out and Mutombo was blocking it. She knew how to defend herself, but Mutombo had learned how to fight in a harder arena that any she had experienced. She scanned the room for a weapon, but there was nothing. She saw him move and raised her arm to protect herself. Her eyes closed tight without any conscious volition.

The attack never came. She opened her eyes and he was still standing in front of her, looking at her with baffled fury. "You think I killed her. You think I went after her like some animal so I could... You think that what I am makes me guilty."

"I think that your phone was close by Farah Jafari's body. That's what makes you guilty."

She sensed movement behind him. Her first thought was that Dave had worked out what was happening and was, somehow, here, then she realised it was Jim Radcliffe, moving quietly forward behind Mutombo. He held something – she recognised the cricket bat from his office in the church – raised, and his hands were tensing for the swing.

"No!" Tina's shout alerted Mutombo who whipped round, straight into the line of the descending bat. The blow caught him at an angle, deflecting its force. He staggered, grabbed at the door frame, then sank onto his knees and rolled onto the floor.

Radcliffe stared at the fallen man, his face white. "Karen said he was attacking you."

"He was. He... Then he didn't. You might have killed him." She went down on her knees and felt Mutombo's pulse. It was beating strongly, but he didn't move.

"Is he OK? I didn't mean to hit him. I..."

"No, he isn't. Call an ambulance. Now." Tina moved him into the recovery position. He was breathing, but there was a stertorous sound to it she didn't like, and a dark bruise was spreading across his forehead. Her mind was working fast as she tended to the injured man.

"You said Karen...?"

He nodded. "She's here. She saw the shelter door was open and came in to see what was happening. She ran down to the church to find me."

Karen Morgan came up behind Jim Radcliffe and looked down at the recumbent form of Andre Mutombo. Her fingers touched Radcliffe's shoulder. "You had to stop him." She knelt down next to Tina. "I'm a trained first-aider," she said.

"I hit him. Andre..." Radcliffe's face was anguished.

Tina scrabbled across the floor to her phone. It was dead. "We need an ambulance," she said. "I need a phone. Where...?"

"The church. That's the nearest." Karen Morgan spoke from where she was crouching on the floor. "Take Jim." Her eyes met Tina's. "He needs to get away from this."

Radcliffe was leaning against the wall, saying over and over, "I thought he was attacking you.

I thought…"

"Come on." Tina grabbed his arm and pulled him out of the shelter. "The church. Get your keys. Hurry."

"I thought… I didn't realise…"

Tina grabbed the bunch of keys he was fumbling with and set off down the road, leaving him in the car park. She didn't have time to take care of Radcliffe. Mutombo was seriously hurt. Radcliffe would have to wait.

It was as if her mind caught up with events as the cold air cleared her head. She could see Andre Mutombo standing in the entrance to his flat, looking at her with cold dislike. *Maybe you should ask the woman. She is the one who chases the men.*

Karen Morgan. Tina had asked for a phone and Karen had sent Tina to the church, even though the phone was on the desk beside her. Somehow, she knew it was dead. She must have a mobile. Jim Radcliffe had a mobile, but she'd sent Tina to the church. She wanted her out of the way. *Maybe you should ask the woman. She is the one who chases the men.*

The woman. Not Farah Jafari, almost a child, struggling to survive, but Karen Morgan with her hungry, yearning gaze fixed on Jim Radcliffe.

Jesus! Tina was running back up the hill, her

legs feeling as though she was running through treacle. Jim Radcliffe was standing in the car park looking bewildered. "The police!" she shouted to him. "Get the police. Now."

And she was into the shelter and at the office door in moments, in time to see Karen Morgan swing the raised bat down with deadly accuracy towards the wound on Andre Mutombo's skull.

Tina threw herself into the room, her hands catching the woman square in the back, knocking her to the floor. Karen Morgan twisted round and was on her feet as the momentum from Tina's leap spun her into the corner.

Tina's head cracked on the desk, and she lay there, dazed. "He recovered and attacked you," Karen Morgan said. "I had to hit him. But he'd already hit you. I was too late." The bat swung back.

Tina knew she had to roll out of the way, cover her head, protect herself from what would be a death blow, but her body wouldn't obey her.

The bat reached the peak of its swing, paused a moment, then...

"Karen!" It was Jim Radcliffe's voice. "Karen! What are you doing?"

And the wood clattered to the ground, and Karen Morgan stood there frozen. Then she folded into Jim Radcliffe's arms, sobbing. "I did it for you," she said. "I did it for you."

***

It was Roy Farnham who came and sat with Tina after she had given her statement. She felt out of place, part of the crime rather than part of the investigation. His hand moved towards her, then dropped. "You OK?" he said abruptly.

"Yes, sir." She suspected she was in trouble, but she was too tired to care.

"We'll make this off the record, Tina. Why didn't you come and talk to me? You know what damage this kind of private sleuthing can do."

"I didn't have anything to tell you. It was just..."

"A hunch? You think I wouldn't have listened to you? Tina, you were on the spot, you know these people. Of course I'd have listened to you."

Karen Morgan had admitted killing Farah Jafari. "She wasn't a refugee, she was just a slut. She was just spinning a line, using him because he cared," she said, her mouth distorted with love and fury as they waited for the police to arrive. She knew that Jim Radcliffe had crossed a line when he helped Jafari to get her papers.

"Once I'd found out what she'd done, I put the fear of God into her. I told her to make herself scarce or she was going into detention. She knew if she came near us again, I'd make sure she was arrested. I'd make sure she was sent back."

She had driven Jim Radcliffe to the shelter the night of the murder, and had seen Jafari in the street close by. She had assumed the girl was on her way to try and get Radcliffe to help her again. "He's too soft with them. He was going to get himself into trouble. I wasn't going to let that happen."

She had followed Jafari in her car, and when the girl vanished into the gennel, presumably looking for somewhere sheltered, she had followed her. "I did what I had to."

"How did Andre Mutombo's phone end up on the scene?" Tina asked Farnham now.

"Mutombo was at Nadifa's House that afternoon. His phone was stolen while he was there. Farah Jafari was trying to get help but she must have been petrified of running into Morgan, or even Radcliffe. She saw an opportunity, took the phone and some money, and ran. It was the phone that guided Amir to her body. He was calling Mutombo back at the centre, and the phone rang. Amir knew Mutombo hadn't killed her, but he knew how bad it looked, so he kept his mouth shut and relied on our famous British justice."

"Which almost didn't work."

"It worked," Farnham said. "Forensics came through. There were finger marks on her neck that didn't come close to matching his."

"So I..." Tina felt like a quixotic fool.

"You speeded things up a bit," Farnham conceded. "And what you found out gave us a line on the girl in the river. I don't know how far we'll get, but at least we know where to look. OK, this is what I wanted to say. Officially, you're out of line. It won't get as far as a reprimand, because I don't want it to. I want you back on the team. If you're going to be around, I'd rather have you inside the tent pissing out than outside pissing in."

And Tina knew that was as close as she was going to get to thanks.

***

It was a week later, and Tina was leaving Nadifa's House after saying her farewells. She was taking up Roy Farnham's offer and going back to the serious crimes unit. Jim Radcliffe was in the office, hovering, wanting to talk to her. She wasn't sure she wanted to talk to him, but she stopped when he came over to her.

"Andre's coming out of hospital today. No permanent damage. I just hope he'll understand."

Tina doubted Mutombo would. For those few minutes, Radcliffe had seen him as a killer. "I'm glad he's OK."

"And we're having a memorial for Farah. Maybe we'll find her family one day. I don't know. I can try." He sighed. "I messed up, didn't I?"

She nodded. She wasn't going to try and make him feel better.

"But Karen. Why? Why would she do that?"

She looked at him. He didn't know. He genuinely didn't know. Love. Jealous, obsessive, compulsive. Love was a dangerous thing, and Tina wanted no part of it.

"Thank you for not... You could have got me into serious trouble."

"No. You got yourself into serious trouble. You need to remember that."

She had to go through the small café as she left the building. Amir was sitting at one of the coffee tables. He stood up when he saw her, bowing slightly, his hand against his chest. "Ma'am. Thank you."

"Why, Amir? I didn't do anything."

"You helped me. You believed in me." His smile was both warm and distant, marking the gulf that lay between them.

"Amir, if you had trusted me..."

"And left my friend in trouble? Ma'am, I could not do that."

She shook her head. He was wrong, but she knew she couldn't alter his unswayable conviction. "What are you going to do now?"

His smile broadened. "I hear today from the immigration. They have accepted I have evidence for a new application. My case is open again."

"I'm glad. Good luck, Amir."

"Thank you ma'am. God bless you."

He would remain in the limbo of the asylum system for years, unable to work, unable to marry, unable to do anything beyond exist, but somewhere and somehow he had found cause for hope.

She walked through the city centre, past the giant Ferris wheel that dominated Fargate, the cobbles uneven under her feet. She cut down past the arched roofs of the Winter Gardens, down the steps towards Arundel Gate. She negotiated her way over the crossings and down the hill towards South Yorkshire Police HQ. Farnham had called her in for a briefing, cutting her leave short. A new case was getting under way.

She showed her security pass at reception, and followed the directions along a corridor that still looked shiny and new. The doors were numbered, but she didn't need to read them. She could hear the sound of voices as the team assembled.

She stood in the doorway looking at the familiar faces. Dave was at the front of the room, waiting for Farnham to start the briefing. He saw her standing there, and grinned. She stepped into the room as heads began to turn.

"I'm back," she said.

Crime Express is an imprint of Five Leaves Publications

www.fiveleaves.co.uk

Other titles include

Trouble in Mind by *John Harvey**
The Mentalist by *Rod Duncan**
The Quarry by *Clare Littleford**
The Okinawa Dragon by *Nicola Monaghan**
Gun by *Ray Banks**
Killing Mum by *Allan Guthrie**
California by Ray Banks
Claws by *Stephen Booth*
Close to the Mark by *Allan Guthrie*
Speaking of Lust by *Lawrence Block*
Graven Image by *Charlie Williams*

* A6 format, with French flaps